More **Dark Man** books:

First series

The Dark Fire ⟨ ... 417-9
Destiny in the ... 422-3
The Dark Neve ... 419-3
The Face in th ... 411-7
Fear in the Dai... ... -412-4
Escape from the Dark   978-184167-416-2
Danger in the Dark   978-184167-415-5
The Dark Dreams of Hell   978-184167-418-6
The Dark Side of Magic   978-184167-414-8
The Dark Glass   978-184167-421-6
The Dark Waters of Time   978-184167-413-1
The Shadow in the Dark   978-184167-420-9

D0537711

Second series

The Dark Candle   978-184167-603-6
The Dark Machine   978-184167-601-2
The Dark Words   978-184167-602-9
Dying for the Dark   978-184167-604-3
Killer in the Dark   978-184167-605-0
The Day is Dark   978-184167-606-7
The Dark River   978-184167-745-3
The Bridge of Dark Tears   978-184167-746-0
The Past is Dark   978-184167-747-7
Playing the Dark Game   978-184167-748-4
The Dark Mus' ... '8-184167-749-1
The Dark Gar ... 8-184167-750-7

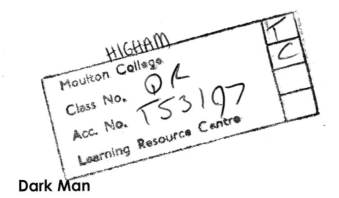

Dark Man

The Dark Side of Magic
by Peter Lancett
illustrated by Jan Pedroietta

Published by Ransom Publishing Ltd.
51 Southgate Street, Winchester, Hampshire SO23 9EH
www.ransom.co.uk

ISBN   978 184167 414 8

First published in 2006
Second printing 2008

Printed in China through Colorcraft Ltd., Hong Kong.

Set 2: Book 2

Dark Man

The Dark Side of Magic

by Peter Lancett

illustrated by Jan Pedroietta

Ransom

Chapter One:
The Girl Knows Magic

The Dark Man follows a girl.

They are in the smart part of the city.

He sees her freeze time.

As the people stand still like statues, she steals from them.

The Dark Man is not frozen.

He knows magic too.

The girl turns and she sees the Dark Man.

It seems as if lights flash before his eyes.

Then he finds himself in a smart flat.

Chapter Two:
Strong Powers

The girl stands before him.

"Did the Old Man send you?" she asks.

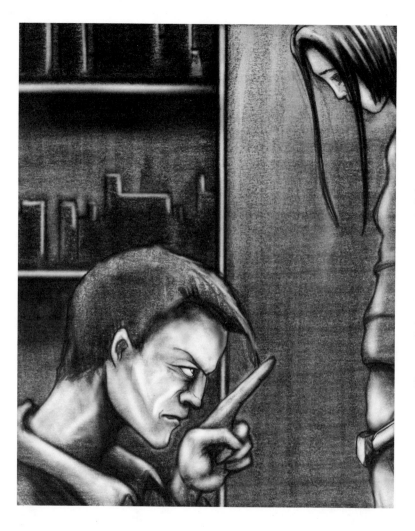

"He cares. He does not want bad things to happen to you."

"What could happen? I have strong powers.

"The Old Man asks me to use them and I help him."

The Dark Man agrees.

"You must learn to control the magic or it will start to control you."

The girl shakes her head.

"Even the Shadow Masters cannot control me," she says.

Chapter Three:
Something Slimy

The Dark Man turns his head sharply.

Something slimy slithers, back into a dark room.

The girl smiles.

"Just my pet," she says.

"Go to see the Old Man," the Dark Man says.

The slimy thing leaps out of the dark room.

The Dark Man turns to fight it.

Chapter Four:
On the Streets

But there is a flash of darkness and he finds himself back on the streets.

He shakes his head.

The Old Man must find the girl now.

He hopes that he will not be too late.

The author

photograph: Rachel Ottewill

Peter Lancett used to work in the movies. Then he worked in the city. Now he writes horror stories for a living. "It beats having a proper job," he says.